ZARA'S
RULES
for
Record-Breaking
FUN

ZARA'S RULES for Record-Breaking FUN

HENA KHAN

Illustrated by Wastana Haikal

SALAAM
READS

NEW YORK | LONDON | TORONTO
SYDNEY | NEW DELHI

SALAAM
READS

An imprint of Simon & Schuster Children's Publishing Division
1230 Avenue of the Americas, New York, New York 10020

For information about special discounts for bulk purchases, please contact Simon & Schuster
Special Sales at 1-866-506-1949 or business@simonandschuster.com.
The Simon & Schuster Speakers Bureau can bring authors to your live event.
For more information or to book an event, contact the Simon & Schuster Speakers Bureau
at 1-866-248-3049 or visit our website at www.simonspeakers.com.
Also available in a Salaam Reads paperback edition
Interior design by Sarah Creech
The text for this book was set in Adobe Caslon Pro.
The illustrations for this book were rendered digitally.
Manufactured in the United States of America
0322 OFF
First Salaam Reads hardcover edition April 2022
2 4 6 8 10 9 7 5 3 1
CIP data for this book is available from the Library of Congress.
ISBN 9781534497597 (hc)
ISBN 9781534497580 (pbk)
ISBN 9781534497603 (ebook)

To Tony, Marion, Michael, and Nomi,

the ultimate neighbors and friends

ZARA'S RULES for Record-Breaking FUN

CHAPTER 1

*** ***

"Someone's going inside!" Zayd yells, his face smooshed against the glass of the front window.

"Is it a family?" Mama rushes over from the kitchen, still holding the head of lettuce she was shredding.

I squeeze next to them to peek through the curtains. We watch an elegant older woman in a suit and heels walk past the FOR SALE sign to the entrance of Mr. Chapman's house.

"I think that's the agent," Mama whispers, as if the lady might hear us from across the street.

"Like a secret agent?" Zayd gasps.

"No, Zayd!" I roll my eyes at my little brother. "A real estate agent, who's selling Mr. Chapman's house."

"It would be cooler if she was a secret agent," Zayd says, before continuing to narrate. "Now there's another car. It's a man and woman, but no kids."

"And hopefully no teenagers?" Baba asks from the stove, where he stirs the spicy meat that's sizzling in a pan.

"What do you have against teenagers?" I flip around to face my father. "You know *I'll* be a teenager in only two years and three months."

"Don't remind me." Baba clutches at his heart and moans.

"Baba! I'm serious."

"Fine. It's not that I don't *like* teenagers," Baba clarifies. He tastes the meat and sprinkles more chili powder on top. "I just don't want any living on our street, driving too fast, having loud parties. And I'd prefer that you and Zayd stay exactly as you are, forever, please."

Mama smiles. "I'm sure Zara and Zayd will be perfect

teenagers when that day comes, eventually, a long time from now, inshallah," she says. She goes back to the kitchen, slides the lettuce into a bowl, and turns the grater on the cheese.

It's Taco Tuesday, so Mama fixes all the toppings while Baba cooks the meat. Today is actually Friday. But Zayd calls *every* night that we have tacos for dinner "Taco Tuesday." I hear my parents tell their friends how adorable that is, over and over again. It was funny the first few times he said it. But now I think it's about time Zayd learns the proper days of the week. I mean, he *is* seven years old already.

I look back out the window. "They're going inside," I share.

"Let me see." Zayd wiggles around for a better view. "I wish kids *my* age would move in," he whines. "It's no fair!"

It's true there aren't any kids on our street who are exactly Zayd's age. But nobody's ten and three quarters like me either, and you don't hear me complaining. We've got little Melvin next door, who's only five. Alan is nine and lives on the other side of us. And Gloria, who's eleven and a half, and her sister, Jade, who's almost thirteen, live next to Mr. Chapman's house.

It's the perfect balance: three boys and three girls, including me and Zayd. We've got our teams for games worked out. Everyone understands and plays by the rules, which took a long time to decide on. And we always have so much fun together. I'd prefer that things stay exactly the way they are.

"No one who moves in will be as nice as Mr. Chapman," Mama sighs, and pops open a jar of salsa. "Or have as beautiful a garden."

I swallow the lump that forms in my throat. Mr. Chapman has always lived across the street, since before I was born. Everyone in our family loves him, and Jamal Mamoo even calls him "the GOAT." I thought my uncle meant the animal and was making fun at first. But then Jamal Mamoo explained that "GOAT" stands for "Greatest of All Time," which makes more sense. Jamal Mamoo is obsessed with sports scores and records and is always talking about who's the best.

The greatest thing about Mr. Chapman is that he pays attention to all of us kids. He gave each of us special nicknames. Mine is "Queen of the Neighborhood," because he said I "rule with grace and fairness." I like the idea of being graceful, especially since my dad teases me about my two left feet. And I'm *really* good at ruling. Even kids who are older than me, like Gloria and Jade, don't mind that I'm in charge. It's probably because I'm so fair.

But Mr. Chapman decided to move to Jacksonville, Florida, because he said he couldn't stand Maryland winters anymore. So the FOR SALE sign went up, and the moving trucks came last week.

"I'm going to grow lemons in Florida," he said during our group goodbye in his driveway. "When you visit, I'll be sure to make the lemonade extra sweet."

I begged him not to move, at least not until winter, but Mr. Chapman said he wanted to give a nice family the chance to move in over the summer. As a parting gift he handed me a small box of Nips. But instead of the chewy caramels that stick to his dentures and my teeth, there was a silver necklace inside. It had a tiny crown charm, which made me smile when I saw it. I tug on it now, and frown, thinking about the people who'll move in next.

Mama seems worried that whoever buys his house won't be able to take care of Mr. Chapman's garden. But I'm nervous about a whole lot more. What if it's someone mean, who yells at us if our ball lands in his yard—instead of telling silly jokes? What if there are new kids who change the feeling of our street? Like the older teens Baba's afraid of, or nasty bullies, or even triplets? How would we make our teams even with triplets?

"Dinner's ready!" Baba interrupts my thoughts. "Can you kids set the table, please?"

Zayd and I look at each other as we leave the window, and I wonder if he's worrying about the same things I am.

"Taco Tuesday is starting!" he yells, grinning, and I realize he's not thinking about it at all.

So I put my worries on pause as I place napkins on the table and fill water glasses. Then I enjoy the feast, which is fit for the Queen . . . of the Neighborhood.

CHAPTER 2

* * *

I squint in the bright sunlight, focusing on Gloria. Gloria pulls back her arm and sends the red ball speeding toward me. I kick it with all my might. And then I sprint to the crab apple tree that's first base.

I grab a low-hanging branch, heavy with tiny apples that are so sour, they make your lips pucker if you dare eat them.

"Safe!" Alan yells as Jade tags me. He waves his arms like an umpire.

"No, she isn't! You have to touch the trunk!" Jade argues.

"The branches are too thick to reach the trunk," I pant. "You can touch *any* part of the tree."

"What about third base, then?" Gloria points to the wooden fence than runs along the side of her yard. "Can you tag the fence anywhere too?"

"No." I kick at a half-rotten apple on the grass. "The fence is so big, that would make it way too easy."

"The tree is also really big," Jade insists.

Sweat rolls off my forehead and down my cheek. The fence is *much* wider than the tree I'm touching.

"How about we make third base the part of the fence with the gate? And first base is only the right side of the tree," I suggest. I'm just trying to rule with grace and fairness—like Mr. Chapman says.

"Fine," Gloria says, and shrugs, living up to the nickname Mr. Chapman gave her: "Ms. Agreeable."

Jade gives me a small nod.

I look around to see if anyone else is protesting, and mop my face with my T-shirt sleeve. Kickball is a serious game on our street, but my rules make sure it's fair.

And our teams are as even as possible: Alan, Melvin, and me versus Gloria, Jade, and Zayd. Right now my team is winning five to three. But Melvin has lost interest and is starting to pick dandelions, and Zayd is so sweaty, it's like he just stepped out of the shower.

"I'm thirsty," Zayd whines. "Can we stop?"

I glance over at Mr. Chapman's porch. Today is especially hot, and some of his lemonade would be perfect right now.

"If we stop now, our team wins," I say, licking my parched lips.

"You always win," Jade grumbles. Her cheeks match the dark pink tank top she's wearing, which she tie-dyed herself last week. Jade is the craftiest out of all of us, which is why Mr. Chapman called her "the Artist." But he pronounced it "ar-*teest*" to be extra fancy, like Jade.

"You won at tag last time," I remind her. "But if you want, we can take a break and run through the sprinkler?"

Jade doesn't respond, because right then a huge truck turns onto our street and stops in front of Mr. Chapman's house. The brakes squeak and the rumbling engine quits.

ACE MOVERS is written in gigantic blue letters across the side.

Gloria turns to me, her eyes almost as huge as her hair poof.

"It's *the New People*," she says.

Suddenly we're all on the same team as we huddle together and gape at the truck. Three men jump out, all wearing weight belts and gloves. They slide open the back of the truck like a garage door. Then they pull down a metal ramp and begin to bring out an assortment of furniture

wrapped in blankets. I search for clues about what kind of people are moving in, but there are no giveaways other than a huge TV box. Whoever these people are, they must enjoy watching TV.

A minivan pulls up next and turns into Mr. Chapman's driveway. Zayd grabs my hand. This is the moment we've been waiting for!

I spot the same man and woman from last night. They get out, hug each other, and stand arm in arm gazing at the house. Then the minivan's side door slides open and a girl and boy tumble out. The boy is tall and lanky, with knobby knees poking out of his shorts and messy dark brown hair. The girl is wearing a striped jumpsuit and sparkly sneakers, and her curly hair is hanging over most of her face.

"They have kids!" Zayd says. He squeezes my hand tighter, and we all continue to watch this family, fascinated, like they're actors starring in a movie.

"How old do you think they are?" Jade whispers.

"The boy's probably my age," Alan says. "And about my height."

"He looks way older than eight, and taller than you," Jade counters.

"I'm nine and a half!" Alan grumbles. "Remember, it was *just* my half birthday?"

"He could be twelve or thirteen," I guess.

The kids pose in front of the house while the lady takes their photo. And then the girl turns her head. I estimate that she's around my age. Her eyes widen as they fall on us.

Without a word we all duck behind the fence, out of sight.

"Why are we hiding?" Melvin chirps after a few seconds.

"I don't know," Jade says, and giggles.

"Should we say hi?" Gloria asks.

I take a deep breath and stand up straight again. The Queen of the Neighborhood fears no one—except for Tala, the big gray husky who lives four doors down and snarls if you get too close to the fence.

The girl is still standing there, facing me, with a curious expression.

13

"Hi," I finally say.

"Hi," she replies with a little wave.

We stare at each other and don't say anything else.

"Naomi! Michael! Come and see your rooms!" the lady who I'm guessing is their mom calls from the front door of the house.

Just like that, the New People turn and run into Mr. Chapman's house and claim it for themselves. And I have no idea what to make of them. I wish the lady who sold them the house actually *was* a secret agent. Then she could have given us some details. But now it's up to me to find out more about our new neighbors.

CHAPTER 3

* * *

"The New People are moving in," I tell Mama and Naano as I burst into the kitchen. They are sitting together at the table, drinking chai. "Same ones from yesterday."

"We saw them from the window," Mama says. "And they have kids after all."

"Too bad Chapman left. He was a good man." Naano shakes her head sadly.

"A very kind chap," Nana Abu adds from the sofa. Then he chuckles at his own joke. My grandparents used to say hello to Mr. Chapman whenever they visited us. Sometimes Nana Abu went on walks with him and sat with him on his porch. When Mr. Chapman left, Naano packed him a cooler of parathas and kabobs, in case he couldn't find any in Florida.

"We should take something over to the new neighbors, to welcome them," Mama suggests.

"Samosas?" Naano says. "I can fry some right now."

"How about cookies?" I ask. "Everybody likes cookies."

Naano wrinkles her nose. "Cookies shookies! They can buy cookies from the store. But not my homemade samosas."

"I want cookies," Zayd says.

"Come here." Naano waves Zayd over to her, and he crawls onto her lap.

"Tell me. What does my skinny mouse want? You need some meat on these bones. I will make you whatever you like," Naano offers.

"Cookies!" Zayd repeats.

Now that Zayd wants them, Naano takes the suggestion

seriously. "Maybe I can make nankhatai. Special Pakistani cookies. Then you can take some to the neighbors, too."

Mama brightens. "Ooh. You haven't made nankhatai in years!"

"Anything my Zaydoo wants," Naano coos. Zayd's so skinny, his arms are like toothpicks, and everyone is obsessed with feeding him. But no one else as much as our grandmother. And Zayd eats it up. The attention, that is. When it comes to food, there are only a few types that he will eat happily: plain rice, plain pasta, plain paratha, plain pizza, chicken nuggets, Cap'n Crunch, and cookies.

"Zara, you help me," Naano orders. "Get me flour, butter, sugar, eggs. Do you have almonds?"

"I think so." Mama fumbles through the pantry.

"And I need elaichi."

"What?" I ask.

"Cardamom!" Naano replies.

Naano always mixes Urdu and English together when she speaks to us. Zayd and I understand her most of the time because we've gotten good at picking out the English words. Like, when she says "light jalao," I know she's asking me to turn on the lights. Or "TV bund karo" means "turn off the TV." It's like a game for us. If we don't understand, we ask "What?" and Naano automatically translates into English without realizing it. But now she's convinced we can speak Urdu, when we really can't.

The nankhatai end up being butter cookies, each with an almond sitting in the middle of it. Right before they go into the oven, I help Naano brush the tops of the cookies with egg yolks, like painting. When the cookies come out of the oven, they have a shiny yellow glaze.

Mama arranges the nankhatai on a plate, covers them with foil, and hands the plate to me.

"Do you want to take these over?" she asks.

My stomach flip-flops a little at the idea of knocking on the New People's door, but I grab the plate anyway. They should probably know who I am. I hold up my head and march out of the house and across the driveway, ignoring the urge to run back home.

When I get to the door, someone opens it before I even knock. It's the woman.

"Well, hello!" The woman's lips stretch into a toothy smile. "You must be our neighbor. Come on in. What's this? Is this for us? How lovely! Thank you so much."

She doesn't stop talking as she takes the plate from my hand and ushers me into the house. I stand in the entryway, unsure what to do next.

"Should I take off my shoes?" I ask, thinking about what I would do in my own house.

"If you'd like. Make yourself at home. Don't mind all the boxes," the woman says, laughing. "It's going to take us a while to unpack. We're the Goldsteins. Where do you live, sweetheart? Naomi! Michael! Come say hello to our new neighbor."

I point to our house across the street while Mrs. Goldstein puts the cookies down on the kitchen counter. Naomi peeks her head out from the hallway upstairs. And then she slinks down the stairs.

"Hi," she says. "What's your name?"

"Zara."

"How old are you?" Naomi circles me, staring at me intently.

"Ten and three quarters. What about you?"

"I just turned ten."

"Oh, how wonderful!" Mrs. Goldstein yells from the kitchen. "You're the same age! Where do you go to school, Zara?"

"Brisk River Elementary School."

"Naomi and Michael will be going to the Jewish Day School, but I'm sure you'll have lots of fun in the neighborhood," Mrs. Goldstein replies.

Naomi nods, like she's deciding what to think about that.

"Who were those other kids?" Naomi asks, which means she saw the rest of the gang when we were hiding.

"Melvin Fu is the cute little one with the spiky hair. Alan Goodman is the other boy. He plays all sports and has three cats. Jade Thomas and Gloria Thomas are sisters. Jade is older, but they act like twins. Except Jade is into fashion and making stuff, and Gloria loves reading and biking. Oh, and then there's Zayd Saleem, my little brother."

"That's a lot of kids," Naomi says, and then falls silent.

"I guess," I say, slipping my shoes back on. "Well, see you later. I hope you like the cookies."

As I leave, I hear Mrs. Goldstein whisper, "See? I told you there'd be nice people living here. You're going to be fine."

And then it hits me. Maybe the New People are as nervous about all of us as we are about them.

CHAPTER 4

***

"What are you doing?" Baba sticks his head out of the pantry as I put on my shoes.

"Going outside," I say.

"Can you take Zayd?" Mama calls out from behind a pile of bottles and jars. She throws one into a bin and grumbles, "How do we have three bottles of expired salad dressing in here?" I don't mention that it really isn't that much of a mystery. She and Baba keep buying them whenever they're on sale.

"Does he have to come?" I ask. "We're going on a bike ride."

Mama comes out of the kitchen. "Please. We're trying to organize, and Zayd's making a bigger mess."

Zayd is sprawled on the floor of the family room, setting up a racetrack for his cars in the middle of the carpet. He's dumped out all the cars and pieces everywhere.

"Come on, Zayd," I mutter.

Zayd doesn't look up. "I'm doing this," he says.

"Mama says you have to come. We'll play a game," I promise.

"Fine." Zayd drops the pieces of the track from his hands back into the pile and shoves the cars to the side.

When we get outside, Gloria is already on her bike at the bottom of our driveway, a new turquoise helmet strapped under her chin.

"Hey, Zara. Ready?"

I point toward my little brother.

"Oh, hi, Zayd." Gloria frowns, knowing this means I have to stay close to home. Zayd doesn't properly know how to ride a two-wheeler yet, since Baba just took off his training wheels last weekend. Plus, he isn't allowed to go past the stop sign.

"Let's play kickball," I suggest.

"Again? We did that yesterday."

"Where's Jade?" I ask.

"Still eating lunch."

"Want to play four square when she's done? Or color with chalk?" I quickly think of anything else fun we could do.

"I guess." Gloria unfastens her helmet, hangs it on her handlebar, and sighs.

"It's so hot out," Zayd complains.

I want to tell him to go back inside then, so I can still go on my bike ride, but I don't. My parents would only get annoyed at me.

The Goldsteins' garage door opens, and Naomi appears. We watch as she rummages through a box and drags something heavy over to the front yard. Then she walks over to where we are.

"Hi," she says.

"Hi," I answer.

"Hi," Gloria adds.

Zayd gives her a nod of acknowledgment.

"Do you have a bike pump I can borrow?" Naomi asks us.

"Yeah, sure. Zayd, can you get her the pump?" I say. "It's next to the paint cans in the garage."

Zayd trots off and returns with the pump. Naomi thanks him and goes back to her yard. Then she starts to inflate a small round kiddy pool with dolphins on it, like the one Zayd had when he was a toddler.

"Do they have a baby brother or sister?" Gloria asks me, looking confused.

"I don't think so," I reply.

After the pool is inflated, Naomi unwinds the hose that Mr. Chapman left at the front of the house. She starts to fill the pool with water.

"I'm making a cool tub," she announces as we watch her.

"A what?" Gloria asks.

"Like the opposite of a hot tub. A cool tub. To cool down in."

Gloria looks at me and raises her eyebrows. I shrug. It's not the worst idea I've ever heard.

"Want to try it?" Naomi offers. "I'm going to put on my bathing suit."

The pool is tiny. I don't see how we'll all fit inside. Plus, we already have plans.

"We were just about to—" I start to say.

"I'll be right back," Gloria interrupts.

She hops onto her bike, rides to her house, and runs inside.

A few minutes later Gloria comes out with Jade. Both of them are wearing swimsuits, and Jade's got on big heart-shaped sunglasses. Just like that, they walk over to Naomi's yard, although they've hardly even *met* Naomi yet. She's practically a stranger!

"I've always wanted a hot tub," Jade says, giggling. "But in August a cool tub is a *way* better idea than a hot tub!"

"Hey!" I call over to them. "Don't you want to play four square?"

"Maybe later," Jade says as she slides into the cool tub. Water pours out onto the lawn, and the girls shriek and splash each other.

Zayd starts to laugh and runs across the street, without looking both ways first.

"Zayd!" I yell. "You have to LOOK. And take off your shoes and socks—"

It's too late. Zayd leaps into the cool tub, sneakers and all.

"Come on, Zara," Naomi calls to me. "We can make room."

Zayd is halfway in Jade's lap, and Gloria's knees are squeezed up to her face. From my lawn it doesn't look like there's any room in there for me.

Michael comes out of his house, surveying the scene with a flavored ice pop in his hand.

"Ooh! Let's have freeze pops while we sit in the cool tub," Naomi shouts. She jumps up and runs into her house, still dripping.

When she comes out again with a handful of the colorful frozen sticks, I walk across the street and take the one she offers me. It's purple. My least favorite flavor. Still, it's cold and refreshing. And when I finally kick off my sandals and dip my toes into the cool tub, I have to admit it feels amazing.

But that still doesn't stop me from noticing how quickly everyone decided to bail on my plans and follow

Naomi. And that feels almost as bad as the brain freeze I suddenly get from the flavored ice. I have to come up with a plan to make sure I stay Queen of the Neighborhood. And fast.

CHAPTER 5

* * *

I race Zayd to the front door when the doorbell rings, but he gets there first.

"It's Jamal Mamoo!" he whoops.

"Salaams, buddy," Jamal Mamoo says. Our uncle comes in balancing a couple of pizza boxes in one hand and carrying a bag in the other.

"Hey, can you grab this, Zara? It's heavy," he warns as I take the bag.

"What is it? Soda?" I guess, hoping. Mama doesn't normally let us drink soda.

"You wish," Jamal Mamoo says. "It's a surprise."

Of course that means Zayd looks inside the bag immediately.

"It's old books!" Zayd's face clouds. "Where's the surprise?"

"The books *are* the surprise."

"Oh."

"Don't look so excited." Jamal Mamoo chuckles, his white teeth parting behind his short beard. "These were mine when I was younger. I found them in a box when I was cleaning. They're some of my favorites."

"Thank you," I quickly say, remembering my manners.

"At least there's pizza," Zayd mutters. He has obviously forgotten his manners.

"Jamal!" Mama greets her younger brother with a hug and takes the pizza boxes out of his hand. "You didn't need to bring this. There's so much food already."

"But we're watching football," Jamal Mamoo says. "There has to be pizza. And besides, Zara and Zayd like it, right?"

"I made your favorite biryani," Naano says, and clucks her disapproval. She carries a big dish of the spicy chicken and rice and a bowl of yogurt to the dining table. "Bring the plates, Zayd," she calls. "And your plain rice."

"You know, preseason doesn't count," Nana Abu says as he shuffles over to the sofa and switches on the TV, with the volume turned up extra loud.

"It's still football," Jamal Mamoo insists. "I've been waiting all summer." He tears off a slice of pizza before getting his plate.

I sit on the arm of my uncle's chair, watching how he folds the slice in half and eats it in three bites. He follows that up with a heaping plate of biryani, all while keeping up with the game, having a conversation with his parents, and making jokes.

My grandparents seem to understand the rules of football pretty well, which is shocking. Naano splits her free time between reading the Quran and watching Pakistani dramas on the special channels she gets at her house. Nana Abu is usually reading, watching cricket and international news, or napping. And yet somehow they both know how many yards make a first down and what "pass interference" is, better than me. Impressive.

"What's up, Zara?" Jamal Mamoo asks me after a moment. "Why do you look so glum? Don't you want some food?"

"In a little bit," I quickly say. I don't want to mention Naomi and the cool tub, so instead I open the bag of books and rifle through them. There's a thick one with shiny lettering on it.

"That's my old book of Guinness World Records." Jamal Mamoo smiles. "I read that thing over and over again. Even tried to break a few records."

"Did you ever break one?" I ask. Maybe this book explains why my uncle is always talking about scores and records and winning and GOATs.

"Nope." Jamal Mamoo shrugs. "But I'm not nearly as talented as you. Although, some of those records are super random, like building the highest tower of toilet paper in thirty seconds. I thought that one seemed easy, but it's way harder than it sounds."

I flip through the pages.

"Eww!" I gawk at a photo of a man holding the record for the longest toenails in the world. His nails are gnarled and twisted like the roots of a tree. "How does this guy walk?"

During halftime the announcers on TV make a big deal about one of the players on the green team. As they flash his photo onto the screen, they discuss all the records he holds and how he dominates his position.

"He's going to break more records this year," Jamal Mamoo says, his voice filled with admiration. "And he's going to the Pro Football Hall of Fame for sure."

A Hall of Fame sounds like an amazing place. I imagine a long hallway with a red carpet and sparkling chandeliers, where people line up to shake your hand and take pictures. This football player isn't even there yet, but on the sidelines his teammates are slapping his shoulders and crowding around him. It's like they know they're near greatness. And it's all because he breaks records.

I turn back to the book on my lap. Maybe this is the way to seal my place as the Queen of the Neighborhood!

I'm going to break a world record. Like Jamal Mamoo said, I'm pretty talented. I've taken a bunch of classes in the past, like tap dancing, kung fu, and basket weaving. Even though I quit them all, I learned some things that could come in handy.

The question is, which record should I break? I inspect my toenails, which are neatly trimmed, and shudder. I'm definitely skipping that one! Whatever I do, I know everyone will be super impressed. Zara Saleem, Guinness World Record breaker. Maybe I can have my very own Hall of Fame, right here in the neighborhood.

Thinking of all the possibilities gets me excited, and hungry.

"Yes!" Jamal Mamoo cheers as his team scores. He gets up and high-fives everyone, and then grabs a pizza box.

"Pass me a slice, please," I say, handing him my plate. I need to fuel up for whatever comes next.

CHAPTER 6

* * *

"Mama!" I yell after rummaging through my closet the next morning. "Do you know where my tap shoes are?"

"No," Mama calls back from downstairs. "Did you check your closet?"

"They're not in there!"

"I don't know, then. I haven't seen them."

It's been a while since I took tap lessons at the community center. I liked it, until my teacher said I needed to work on my rhythm and kept coming over to help me individually. She told me I was doing a "great job," but the way she said it through gritted teeth made it seem like she didn't mean it.

I finally find the black shoes under my bed, behind a box full of my old art projects. The shoes are covered with dust, which I brush off. And although they're a little tight, I manage to squeeze my feet into them and fix the strap. Ta-da!

When I looked through Jamal Mamoo's book, I found a few records about tap dancing, like the highest number of taps per minute and the longest distance traveled while tap dancing. But I picked the record for longest time spent tap dancing without stopping to break—seven hours and thirteen minutes. I'm going to tap for seven hours and *fourteen* minutes

My tap dance lessons ended over a year ago, and I'm not sure how much I'll remember. But once I strap on the shoes, the shuffle hop step comes right back to me. The problem is, I can't hear anything but a dull thumping on my carpet.

Thump-thump, thump, THUMP! Thump-thump, thump, THUMP!

So I go downstairs to the kitchen, where the floors are smooth and hard.

Mama is in here with my grandparents. They just got back from Halalco, all the way in Virginia, which Naano thinks is too far away for Nana Abu to drive. My family loves going there, since you can find stuff Muslims like to buy. Last time I went, we came back with a car full of lamb chops, halal bologna, a huge box of dates, Ramadan decorations, and a jumbo Arabic alphabet floor puzzle.

"I see you found your shoes," Mama says. "Want some?" She pushes a container of dried apricots toward me.

"Are you going to dance for us?" Nana Abu asks.

"If you want, but I don't remember that much," I warn.

"Why don't you show us a few steps?" Mama asks.

I know how much my grandparents like to see us perform, so I stand extra tall, extend my arms, and demonstrate the shuffle hop step.

Tap-tap, tap, TAP! Tap-tap, tap, TAP!

Tap-tap, tap, TAP! Tap-tap, tap, TAP!

Tap-tap, tap, TAP! Tap-tap, tap, TAP!

"Very nice." Nana Abu beams and claps for me when I stop.

"Very loud." Naano plugs her ears with her fingers. "Can you do it quieter?"

"That's kind of the point," Mama says, laughing. "But why the sudden interest in tap dance, Zara?"

"I'm going to break the world record for the longest time tapping without stopping."

"Oh." Mama's eyes grow bigger, and then she exchanges a worried look with Naano.

"Where?" Naano asks with a grimace. "Not in here, right?"

"Yeah, here. I need to do it where the floor is hard, Naano."

"How about outside?" Naano points to our driveway, then across the street. "Actually, maybe go to Chapman's driveway."

"My shoes will get ruined!" I protest. "It's too rough.

I can't do it on the driveway. Can I do it inside? Mama, please?"

Mama turns to Naano and gives her a nod that means she'll handle the situation. In this case I know I'm the situation. But I don't understand what the problem is. Since when did practicing a hobby and breaking a world record become a bad thing?

"How about the garage? You can put down that big piece of cardboard and tap on that?" Mama suggests. "That way you'll muffle the sound and not disturb anyone, but you'll still hear a tap."

Zayd is in the other room playing with an electronic toy garbage truck. It's making high-pitched beeps alternating with fake trash-grinding sounds. He's disturbing everyone way more than me, but as usual Naano doesn't mind his noise. I swallow the bitter feeling rising inside me and tap my way over to the garage door. I'll show all of them when I break the record.

The cardboard seems like a good idea at first. I drag it over to the empty part of the garage, lay it flat, and stand on it. But soon after I start tapping on it, it starts to flatten and tear. Plus, it slides around.

"Whoa!" I yell when I almost wipe out. I also forgot to start timing myself.

Zayd peeks his head out the door. "What are you doing?" he asks.

"Breaking a record. Can you help me?" I ask.

"What do I have to do?" Zayd eyes the scene in front of him suspiciously. "I'm not dancing."

"Just time me. And make sure no one interrupts."

"Okay."

I show Zayd where to press the timer.

"Ready? On your mark, get set, go!" he says.

I start to tap my heart out.

Tap-tap, tap, TAP! Tap-tap, tap, TAP!

Tapping on the smooth concrete makes a satisfying sound. But it also hurts my feet. It doesn't help that my toes are squished into the shoes. After a while I can feel a blister forming. And my shins start to burn.

"Good job, Zara," Zayd encourages.

"How long has it been?" I pant.

"Three minutes and thirty-seven seconds."

"That's it?" It feels like forever. "Can you get me some water? With a straw?"

Zayd returns with half a glass of lukewarm water and a bendy straw. He puts it near my mouth, and I try to drink while still tapping. The straw almost goes up my nose, and as I sip, I start to cough and sputter.

"Eww! You sprayed me!" Zayd wipes his face with his sleeve.

The door to the garage opens again. It's Mama.

"Zara! I asked you to do that on the cardboard. Naano and Nana Abu are resting, and that's still too loud."

"But I'm getting close to setting the record!" I argue. "Zayd, how long now?"

"Seventeen minutes and forty-nine seconds."

"That's it?"

"Zara, please, do this later," Mama says firmly.

"Okay."

I stop, because she asked me to. And also because I can't feel my feet anymore. I'll just have to find another way to break a record.

CHAPTER 7

* ✳ *

The next day I come up with a new, and better, plan. I'm going to make the longest sidewalk chalk drawing in history! Baba bought us a fresh tub of sidewalk chalk last time we went to the grocery store, plus there's an extra bucket of broken pieces we've collected over the years in the garage. I'll be super quiet while I draw, so no one can complain about noise. And I mostly need to use my hands and arms, which helps, since my feet are still sore.

It's a sunny and hot day, like it's been all week. I put on a hat, fill a bottle with ice water, and head outside. When the grown-ups go for walks in the neighborhood, the loop they take around the block measures exactly a half mile. So I just need to go around it twice, and I'll have an entire mile of chalk art!

I decide to draw a big rainbow zigzag on the sidewalk. It looks like the top of a crown, which seems right for the Queen of the Neighborhood. The chunky chalk glides smoothly over the concrete and feels good.

I'm working on my seventh square of sidewalk when Naomi comes outside. She's holding a few beanbags and starts to toss them into the air. I think she's trying to juggle them, but she keeps dropping the bags.

"What are you doing?" She walks over to me and looks over my shoulder while I draw. A beanbag falls near my foot.

"Making a design."

"What for?"

"Just because." I feel a slight pang of guilt for hiding my goal of breaking the world record. But I want to do it first and tell people afterward.

"That's nice. I like the rainbow," Naomi says. "Want some help?"

"Well, I kind of want to see how far I can go by myself." If I let Naomi join me, then it won't be just me breaking the record. I'd have to share the title, and the Hall of Fame, with her.

"That's okay." Naomi skips away toward Gloria and Jade's house. She knocks, and Jade opens the door.

"Hey, Naomi."

"Hey. Want to play?"

"I'll be right out."

Jade opens up her garage, and she and Gloria both come outside.

"Want to go for a bike ride?" I hear Gloria ask.

"We could, if you want. But I was thinking we could make a clubhouse."

"A clubhouse?" Gloria sounds intrigued. So am I.

"Yeah." Naomi points. "My dad said we can clean up that old toolshed on the side of my house and play in it."

"I've always wanted a tree house! That's kind of like a tree house," Gloria says.

"How dirty is it?" Jade wavers. "It sounds like a lot of work."

48

"It's not that bad," Naomi says. "Mostly cobwebs and leaves. You can look at it first."

"I'll get a broom," Gloria volunteers.

I wipe sweat off my face, take a sip of my water, squint at my chalk, and keep coloring. But it's hard to stay focused as everyone rushes to take part in another one of Naomi's big ideas.

"Hey, Zara!" Gloria yells as she marches by with a broom in hand. "Are you coming to make the clubhouse?"

I pause and start to imagine sitting in the clubhouse, giggling and sharing secrets with the girls, and hanging up a big sign that says PRIVATE: NO SNOOPING. But then I force myself to snap out of it. I have a world record to break! I survey the work I've done already. I've covered a bunch of blocks and almost reached Alan's house. The zigzags are bold and bright.

"Maybe in a little while," I yell back. "I'm doing this right now."

"Oh. Okay," Gloria says. I can hear the confusion in her voice.

I try to ignore the sounds of the girls laughing as they

clean the clubhouse. It gets louder when they start scream-ing because of a giant spiderweb.

"Girls," Mrs. Goldstein calls out from her side door. "I have an old tablecloth you can use. And some Girl Scout cookies for you."

My stomach growls, and I take another sip of my water. It's getting hotter by the minute, although thick clouds have blocked the sun.

Jade runs back and forth from the clubhouse to her house. "I got some string lights. They'll make the club-house pretty, and we can use it at night!" she yells.

Baba comes outside on a work call, wearing his head-phones and talking loudly about something boring. He checks out my giant zigzag and gives me a thumbs-up. And then he goes to the side of the house and starts to put the patio chair cushions into a storage box.

Suddenly a big drop of water falls onto my arm. I look around, and my water bottle is still standing in place. Then there's another heavy drop that falls onto the sidewalk next to me.

PLINK!

I watch with dread as more drops fall onto my art.

PLINK! PLINK! PLINK! And then there's the unmistakable rumble of thunder. There is about to be a storm.

"We'll come back later," I hear Jade promise as she and Gloria run to their house, shielding their hair from the raindrops with their hands.

There's no way to save my drawing. Maybe I could try to cover it up with trash bags, but as the wind picks up, I know it's too late.

BOOM! A clap of thunder sends me scurrying into the house as sheets of rain hit the ground. I stare outside through the window as all my hard work washes into the gutters, along with my hopes of breaking the record.

CHAPTER 8

* * *

The rain pounds against the windows, and the big tree in the yard bends in the howling wind. Its branches brush against the roof, making me jump from the noise.

"Shouldn't we go down to the basement?" I ask my parents, who are both working on their laptops and acting like nothing major is happening.

"Why?" Baba asks without looking up.

"Because of the storm," I say. It's not that I'm afraid of thunderstorms. I got a book from my school's book fair last year that explains all kinds of extreme weather. It's actually tornados that I'm terrified of, ever since I watched *The Wizard of Oz* at Naano's house with Jamal Mamoo when I was little.

"I think we're fine," Mama says absently, and takes a sip of her chai.

Jamal Mamoo told me that what happened in the movie was totally possible. That your house could actually get picked up and carried away by a tornado. Naano got annoyed at him and told me, "Don't listen to that bakwaas." She said that, after living in Maryland for more than forty years, she'd never experienced a tornado. I know Jamal Mamoo was probably teasing me, but I still get freaked out by the idea. And I can't control my imagination.

"Come on, Zayd," I say to my brother, who is playing in his room. "Let's go to the basement. It's safest there."

"We aren't safe?" Zayd's eyes grow huge. "What's going to happen to us?"

"Nothing, Zayd." I don't say anything about being twisted all the way to Oz. "Just bring the flashlights."

We head down the creaky stairs to the basement. The lights flicker for a moment, and Zayd grabs my arm.

"It's fine, Zayd," I reassure him.

"What if the power goes out?" he asks.

"That's why we have the flashlights."

"Oh."

Zayd sits on the edge of the worn sofa and hugs himself, his eyes rounder than usual. "What do you want to do?"

"Let's make a clubhouse." Naomi doesn't have to be the only one who has one.

"You mean like a fort?"

"Yeah."

"Okay!" Zayd perks up, and we pull a few old chairs around the sofa. Then we drape a bunch of colorful shawls and long printed scarves, abandoned from Mama's old shalwar kameez collection, over the tops. We crawl into the tented space. It's quiet, peaceful, and cozy, especially when we turn on the flashlights.

"Want to tell scary stories?" I ask. Forts and clubhouses

are the perfect places to huddle together when you feel safe, and then scare each other.

"No way!" Zayd says. "If you scare me, I'm going upstairs."

"What do you want to do, then?"

"I'm hungry," Zayd says.

I wish we had planned for snacks, like Mrs. Goldstein. Isn't it lunchtime yet? I hear footsteps in the kitchen upstairs and wonder if anyone remembers that they need to feed us.

"We can go up, after we pick something else for me to do to break a world record."

"How about you live in this fort forever and never leave?" Zayd suggests.

"Never?" I snort.

"Not until you break the record for living in a fort. We could bring you food. And pillows. And books."

"But I'd have to use the bathroom," I argue.

"Right." Zayd nods thoughtfully. "You could use a bucket."

"Gross, Zayd! I would never do that. Come on, help me think of something I can do for real. What are some things that I'm good at?"

Zayd is silent as he thinks. And thinks. When he frowns like he's completely stumped, I feel my cheeks heat up.

"Come on, Zayd," I snap. Maybe I should give up on this goal.

"You're good at everything, Zara," Zayd finally says. He looks right into my eyes and smiles like it's the truest thing he's ever believed.

Suddenly I want to hug him. Sometimes little brothers are the best. But even if his words make me feel better, they still don't help me decide what to do next.

"The storm must be over by now," I say. "Let's go eat."

As we file out of the fort, I spot something on the ground, tucked halfway under a toy bin.

"Look, Zayd!" I point.

"My robot!" Zayd cheers. He runs to the bin and pulls out a remote-controlled toy that is missing an arm.

"No! Behind that."

"Where?"

I walk over and pull out my Hula-Hoop. It used to light up when you spun it around, but that part stopped working a while ago. It's still perfectly round, though. And I remember how I got really good at hooping last summer. I felt like I could do it forever.

I step into it, lift it up to my waist, and give it a twirl. I'm still good at it!

This is it. This is the record I'm going to break. I can feel it. I imagine walking into the clubhouse and seeing the shocked and admiring looks on all the kids' faces when I announce that I hold the Guinness World Record for Hula-Hooping.

I'm so excited, I reach out and give Zayd that hug. He's surprised at first. But then he hugs me back, and we run upstairs.

CHAPTER 9

* * *

This time around I'm fully prepared to make my record-breaking go smoothly. I checked the weather, and it's not raining again until next week. It's a bit cooler after yesterday's storm, which helps too. I've got a water bottle and snacks for when I get thirsty and hungry. I've picked out comfortable shoes, and clothes that won't get in the way of my Hula-Hooping: a hat, long shirt, and leggings. Plus, I have music on Baba's portable speaker to keep me going.

Naano and Nana Abu came over a little while ago to

bring us some fresh kabobs they made with the meat from the butcher shop. There's one plate for all of us, and a separate plate of onion-free kabobs for Zayd.

Now Naano is making chutney to go with them, with some of the mint Mama planted on the side of the house. Zayd picked a bunch of it for her before he left with Baba for his swimming lesson, and she blended the fresh leaves with chili peppers and tomatoes. It's so spicy, she keeps smacking her lips and saying "Whoo!" when she tastes it. I skip the watery green chutney, douse my kabobs with ketchup, and grab my hoop when I'm done eating.

"Bye, Naano." I wave as I head outside. My grandmother scans my outfit and the Hula-Hoop and stops me.

"What are you doing? Going for exercise?" she asks.

"Yeah." I pause and then add, "Outside, so you won't hear me."

"Mujhe try karne dho." Naano holds out her hand.

"You want to . . . *try* my Hula-Hoop?"

"Yes. Give it to me."

To my surprise, Naano carries my Hula-Hoop to the

middle of the family room. Then she holds it over her head, slips it around her belly, and spins it like a pro. She wiggles her hips and gets it to rotate a few times before it drops to her knees and then to the floor.

"Ooof! I forgot how to do it," she says with a laugh.

"You knew how before?" This is more and more surprising by the minute.

"When your mother was young, I could do it for longer than her!" Naano winks at me.

"Wow." I try to picture a younger version of Naano doing more than shuffling around the house, cooking, praying, and watching her favorite dramas. It's really hard.

"Here you go. Have fun." She steps out of the hoop and motions for me to pick it up off the carpet. Naano doesn't like bending to the ground anymore, which is why I can't imagine her being a Hula-Hoop champ of any kind.

"Thanks, Naano. I'm going to break the world record," I say as I head out the door. But Naano is already talking to Mama about something else.

Once I'm on the driveway, I set up my water bottle,

turn on some upbeat bhangra music, start my timer, and then begin to Hula-Hoop. I'm determined to go for six hours without stopping and can already see the head-lines: ALMOST-11-YEAR-OLD HULA-HOOPS FOR SIX HOURS, BREAKS RECORD, AND ENTERS HALL OF FAME. I feel great, and the pulsing dhol from the speaker helps me get a good rhythm going.

Alan comes outside wearing a jersey and holding a soc-cer ball a few minutes later. He gives me a nod, like I'm not doing anything out of the ordinary. Then he starts to juggle the ball with his feet. He bounces it off his knees, feet, and chest.

"How many times can you do that in a row?" I ask him without stopping.

"My record is twenty-five touches, but I'm trying to get to fifty."

"What's the world record?"

"I don't know. Some people can do it hundreds of times," Alan says.

"But not kids your age."

"I've seen a kid on my team juggle a hundred times."

"Oh. Well, then I guess you can keep practicing."

"Thanks." Alan snorts.

I don't mention that I'm about to break a record. It doesn't seem nice to rub it in, especially since the next few times, Alan doesn't get more than seven or eight touches before dropping the ball. But then Melvin appears and wants to play. So he and Alan start to kick the ball back and forth.

The Hula-Hoop is spinning smoothly, and I hardly have to move my body to keep it in motion. Every now and then it starts to slow down, and I give it a little nudge with my hip to speed it up again. If it's this easy, I might be able to continue for seven hours!

"What are you doing?" Gloria walks to the mailbox at the end of her driveway.

"Hula-Hooping."

"Yeah, but why?" Gloria surveys my setup, puts her hands on her hips, and stares at me, waiting for an answer. And although I wasn't planning on telling anyone until *after* breaking the record, I blurt out, "I'm going to break the world record."

"Really?" Gloria crosses the street, still holding the mail she took out of the box.

"Yeah. I want to be in the next Guinness World Records book."

"ARE YOU SERIOUS? That would be so AMAZING!" Gloria shouts. As she waves her arms in excitement, some of the mail falls out of the pile, and a gigantic Bed Bath and Beyond coupon lands near my foot. "Guys! You hear that? Zara is breaking a record!"

"Are you going to be famous?" Melvin runs over to me. Alan picks up the ball and follows him. They stand around me and watch.

I start to sweat. This is suddenly much more pressure, and a bigger audience, than I expected.

The Goldsteins' front door opens, and Naomi and Michael come outside. I take a deep breath and keep on Hula-Hooping, like before. But the sun suddenly feels a lot brighter. And as they start to head over, I taste my kabob again and fear I might throw up. My head is spinning like my Hula-Hoop. What's happening to me?

CHAPTER 10

✳ ✳ ✳

"Zara, what's the matter?" Gloria asks.
She peers into my face as closely as she can without bumping into the Hula-Hoop that's still rotating around me.

"It looks like she's about to pass out," Michael says.

"Maybe you should stop, Zara," Alan says. "Forget the record."

"Record? What record?" Naomi asks, coming closer to me.

I straighten my spine, wipe my brow, and keep hooping.

"I'm breaking the world record for Hula-Hooping

without stopping," I say. As soon as the words are out of my mouth, I feel better. It was probably just nerves. I'm not going to throw up, pass out, or stop. I'm going to break this record. And nothing is going to get in my way!

"How long have you been going for?" Naomi scrunches up her face at me.

"Check the timer," I say.

"Wow! Thirty-seven minutes!" Gloria announces.

"Without stopping once?" Michael's eyebrows go up, and I can tell he's impressed.

"Yup."

Michael points to the soccer ball Alan is holding. "Want to play?"

"Sure," Alan says.

"Can you guys go into your backyard?" Naomi asks Alan. "Don't kick the ball here. What if you bump into Zara by accident?"

"I'm watching her break the record," Melvin says.

"Watching is making me dizzy," Michael says. "But

good luck." And then he and Alan walk away.

"Why are you breaking a record?" Naomi asks. "Are you, like, on a team or something?"

"No. Just because," I say after deciding that's not really a lie.

"Have you done it before?" Naomi asks.

"Hula-Hoop? Yeah. This isn't my first time."

"No, I mean break a record."

Does Naomi think people go around breaking records every day?

"I'm trying to set a Guinness World Record. It's kind of a big deal."

"That's so exciting! We can keep you company," Naomi offers. "And help you."

"Oh. Um. Thanks."

"Do you want your water?" Melvin tries to be helpful right away.

"Sure," I say, as Melvin stretches out his tiny arm and gingerly hands me the squeeze bottle. I manage to take a few sips without slowing down and then toss the bottle

back to him. It falls onto the grass near Naomi, and she quickly brushes it off and stands it up.

"You're at forty-three minutes!" Gloria squeals after checking the timer again. "Almost an hour already. Jade won't want to miss this." She dashes back to her house to get her sister. I haven't even broken the record yet, but it's working already! I'm starting to feel like the Queen of the Neighborhood again.

Jade comes out flapping her hands to dry her sparkly silver nail polish while everyone fills her in. Someone announces every time another minute passes. Listening to them chatter does help the time go by. And with the lively music in the background, it feels like a party.

"So, I have all these new ideas for the clubhouse," Jade shares. "We could have a spa day—do our nails and braid our hair and stuff."

"Sure," Naomi says. "Or we could make things."

"Like pottery?" Gloria chimes in. "I've always wanted to make mugs. Or baskets."

Baskets? Gloria knows I took basket weaving! And we've talked forever about making mugs and painting them!

"All of that sounds good," Naomi says.

"Want to finish decorating the clubhouse?" Jade asks. "I think my nails are dry enough."

"What about Zara?" Naomi asks.

"She's got hours to go. We'll come back and check on her soon."

"Need anything else, Zara?" Gloria asks me. "Want more water?"

"I'm good," I say, trying to act casual even though their conversation is making my thoughts start to swirl. Why are my friends in such a hurry to leave already? Isn't this exciting enough?

"It's your dad!" Gloria points as Baba's car turns onto our street and heads toward our driveway. I forgot that he'd be coming home after Zayd's lesson.

"He can't pull into the driveway! Can you move without stopping, Zara?" Naomi asks.

"I'll tell him," Jade volunteers. She walks over to the car, and Baba rolls down the window.

"Hi, Jade."

"Hi, Mr. Saleem. Do you think you can park on the

street? Zara's breaking the world record and can't move."

"Oh, is she now?" I can't see Baba's face but hear in his voice that he's smiling. "Sure."

A few moments later Baba comes up the driveway, after checking our mailbox. Zayd is in his swimming trunks behind Baba, dragging his wet towel on the ground. My father glances at the timer.

"Fifty-two minutes? Seriously? Good job, Zara!"

"Thanks," I manage to say. But it's getting harder to speak. I'm saving all my energy to keep hooping for at least five more hours.

Zayd runs into the garage and brings out his bike.

"Don't bother them, Zayd," Baba warns as he rifles through our mail.

"I'm not! I'm going to ride until I'm dry."

"And then come inside and eat lunch, okay?" Baba says.

"Okay," Zayd agrees as he perches on the bike seat and watches me.

"Oh, look!" Baba holds up something bright. "Mr. Chapman sent a postcard from Florida."

I glance at the card and make out a palm tree, but my attention is still on the girls. They turn their backs and start to walk to Naomi's yard, leaving me with Melvin and Zayd. I can't tell if the twisting in my gut is from disappointment or all the hooping.

Zayd straps on his helmet and starts to pedal his bike up and down the driveway. He looks good, but after a few rotations he starts to wobble. And then it's like I'm watching in slow motion as his bike heads toward me. Zayd's mouth drops open and his eyes squeeze shut at the moment when his front wheel smashes into my Hula-Hoop.

The dented hoop slips down to my legs and lands on my sneakers.

"ZAYD!" I scream as he keeps wobbling on the bike, before falling into the grass. "HOW COULD YOU?"

Melvin immediately starts to cry and runs home. Zayd stares at me in shock and tries to stand his bike up.

Gloria comes back and starts to pat me on the shoulder, but I shove her hand off. Then I kick the dented hoop out of the way and storm into the house, as hot tears of anger fill my eyes.

CHAPTER 11

* * *

"Zayd ruined everything!" I fume, and stomp into the kitchen. Mama and Naano look up, startled. Baba is taking a bite of kabob and puts down his fork.

"What happened?" he asks.

The door flings open behind me, and Zayd runs inside, crying loudly. He races past everyone, jumps onto the sofa next to Nana Abu, and buries his face in the pillows.

"Zara?" Mama gets up and comes over to me. "What's going on?"

"What did you do to him?" Naano asks. She shakes her head at me and follows Zayd to the couch.

"*Me?* I didn't do anything to him!" I yell.

"Zara, watch your tone," Mama warns.

"She always takes *his* side!" I complain. "He came out of nowhere and crashed into me. And I was at fifty-six minutes of Hula-Hooping."

"He ran into you? On purpose?" Baba's face is stern, and he crosses his arms.

I think about the question. "Not totally on purpose. But he wasn't careful. And he didn't need to ride his bike right then. I was getting closer to breaking the world record, and he ruined it!"

"So, that's what this is all about? Breaking another world record?" Mama looks at Baba, and the edges of her lips turn up ever so slightly. Baba bites his lip and glances down at his plate. Wait. Are they . . . *laughing at me?*

"It's not funny!" I shout.

"Zara." Mama's smile is quickly replaced with a frown. "This is no reason to get so worked up. I'm sure it was an accident."

"Have you ever Hula-Hooped for an hour? It's hard work!"

"I Hula-Hooped before," Naano says. "I know you can do it again. But be nice to bechara Zaydoo. He feels bad, right?"

And then my grandmother opens up her arms and Zayd falls into them, sobbing like he's the victim. And then he actually has the nerve to peek at me and slowly blink his big eyes, wet eyelashes and all.

I open up my mouth to say something harsh, but Mama gives me a warning look. So instead I leave and go downstairs to be alone.

When I get there, the fort Zayd and I made is still standing in the middle of the room. Who wants a clubhouse with a kid brother who messes everything up? I kick it all down, which makes me feel powerful and is totally satisfying at first. But after all the shawls and blankets are in a heap on the floor, and I see our stash of books, flashlights, and Zayd's emergency toys, I only feel worse. I plop down onto a pile of pillows and bury my face in my arms. Then I hear footsteps on the stairs. It's probably Zayd, pretending to look for something but really spying on me.

"Go away, Zayd!" I yell. "I'm not talking to you."

"What about me?" It's Jamal Mamoo's voice.

"You're here?"

"I think so. Let me check." Jamal Mamoo enters the basement, pulls out his phone, flips to the camera, and takes a picture of himself. Then he walks over and shows me the picture. He's making a goofy face, and it makes me laugh a little, even though I don't want to.

"I mean, what are you doing here?" I ask.

"Well," Jamal Mamoo says, and he sits on the sofa and stretches out his long legs. "I heard there were kabobs. And I wanted to see how you are doing."

"I'm fine," I say.

"Are you sure? Because a whole bunch of people upstairs warned me not to come down here. One of them had all this snot on his face from crying. It was pretty disgusting."

I assume he's talking about Zayd.

"He's being such a baby! Zayd bumped into me when I was Hula-Hooping. And, Mamoo, I was starting to get close to breaking the Guinness World Record. I was at fifty-six minutes!"

Jamal Mamoo gasps.

"Are you serious? Fifty-six minutes? That's incredible!"

"I know."

"That little twerp! I should go wipe that snot off his face right now. How could he do that to you? His only older sister! He's trying to destroy you!"

I can't tell if Jamal Mamoo is serious or not.

"He didn't do it on purpose," I admit.

"So what? He still ruined everything."

"Yeah. I guess."

"I'm telling you. Little brothers are the absolute worst. Just ask your mom. She'll say the same thing about me."

"Not you. You're the GOAT, mamoo."

Jamal Mamoo grins. "I know."

"Zara!" I hear Mama's voice from the top of the stairs. "Your friend is here to see you!"

Jamal Mamoo turns to me.

"A friend? We'd better get up there quick, before someone eats my kabobs."

CHAPTER 12

✳ ✳ ✳

The "friend" is actually Naomi, and she's standing on the front step when I come to the door.

"Here's Zara," Mama says to her as I approach. "You're welcome to come play inside if you'd like."

Mama is holding a plate covered in plastic wrap. "Naomi brought back our plate, and made us some cookies," she tells me. "Isn't that nice?"

"My mom made them," Naomi clarifies.

"Well." Mama smiles. "Whoever made them, it's still very nice."

"Did you say cookies?" Nana Abu shuffles to the door. He takes the plate out of Mama's hand and reaches under the plastic. "They look like mini croissants."

"It's rugelach," Naomi says. "Half of them have jam inside, and the other half are chocolate."

"Rug-ooh-la. Mmm. Hmm." Nana Abu nods his approval with his mouth full. "Jam's good. Let's try chocolate now."

"Abu!" Mama warns. "That's a lot of sugar."

"Rug-ooh-la," Naano repeats as she comes to survey the goods. "They are pretty. Speaking of pretty, did you like my nankhatai?"

"Yeah, they were really yummy too," Naomi says. But I can tell by the way she shrinks away from the door that there are probably too many grown-ups staring at her. So I step outside and close the door behind me.

"Are you okay?" Naomi asks when we're alone. She pushes stray curls out of her face, and her eyes are filled with sympathy.

"Yeah."

"Are you really mad at your brother?"

"Yeah." I don't mention that I'm also mad at my grandmother for taking his side. And while I'm at it, at Gloria and Jade, too, for picking Naomi over me.

Naomi turns and disappears behind the bush for a moment. When she reappears, she's holding my Hula-Hoop.

"I tried to fix it," Naomi says, holding it out to me. "But it's still a little bent."

There's a pinch in my chest. I've been trying to hide my record-breaking plans from her and getting annoyed because everyone likes her ideas. And here she is, being nice to me.

"Thanks," I mumble. I slip the Hula-Hoop back around my waist and give it a spin. It mostly works but catches in the spot where it's bent.

"Are you going to try again?" Naomi asks.

"I don't know." I sigh. I'm starting to wonder if I'm not cut out for record-breaking after all. Maybe I shouldn't have quit so many of the activities I tried in the past. Maybe if I was one of those wonder-kids who plays piano concertos at age four, or a super child athlete, it would be easier. What if Jamal Mamoo was only being nice when he called me talented, and I actually don't have what it takes to get more than a participation trophy, let alone into a Hall of Fame?

"If you try again, you should set up cones all around you," Naomi suggests. "We have some packed somewhere."

"Yeah, maybe." Although, I doubt cones could have stopped the two-wheeled terror named Zayd from bumping into me.

Naomi starts to go down the steps. "I have to check the oven. I'm trying to break the world record for baking the biggest rugelach ever." She drops this last piece of information super casually.

"What?" I ask, hoping I heard wrong.

"It's in the oven now. Do you want to help me measure it, to make sure it wins?"

I can't believe it. Naomi is totally copying me! And worst of all, she isn't the slightest bit embarrassed about it. Here I was, beginning to think maybe she wasn't so bad.

"I thought it would be cool if we all broke records. Then we can be in the book together," Naomi adds.

No, no, no! That is *not* the way this is supposed to go.

"So, you're telling me that *you're* trying to break a record too?" I challenge.

"Yeah." Naomi shrugs. "Why not? You inspired me."

"Oh." I guess I can see how I could be pretty inspiring.

"I have to check on the rugelach." Naomi raises an eyebrow. "You coming?"

Since I don't know what else to do, I follow her, dragging my Hula-Hoop behind me. My thoughts are all jumbled up like ingredients in a mixing bowl, but I am curious about this giant cookie.

When we walk into the house, the air smells like a bakery, with hints of cinnamon and warm butter. Naomi checks the timer on the oven.

"Four more minutes," she says.

The counter of the kitchen is covered with bags of flour, sugar, jam, and other ingredients.

"Let's see it," I say with a sigh.

"Here it is." Naomi turns on the oven light, and I peer inside.

"Is it supposed to be totally flat like that?" I ask. "And all bubbly and brown?"

"What?"

Naomi puts on an oven mitt and opens the oven door. A blast of heat fills the room. And then there's a loud wail. From Naomi.

"Moooooom!" she cries. "Something is wrong with the rugelach."

Mrs. Goldstein appears quickly, like she was waiting to come in and rescue the cookie. She grabs the oven mitt, takes out the pan, and shakes her head.

"This doesn't look right. Are you sure you measured correctly?"

"Yes! I did everything the way the recipe said. I cut the butter and the cream cheese and mixed it with the flour in the food processor. And then I rolled out the dough. I added the cinnamon and nuts and folded it like an envelope."

I have to admit, it sounds like Naomi worked hard on this.

"Well, I think you overbaked it. It looks like a sheet cake now." Mrs. Goldstein pokes it with a knife. "Or maybe a cracker."

"It's supposed to be a rugelach! Now I'm not going to break the record." Naomi's face droops, and I can taste her

disappointment.

"It might still be good." Mrs. Goldstein breaks off a small corner of the cake and pops it into her mouth. Her face changes as she chews, from surprise at first to something like disgust. And then she turns to us and grimaces.

"Or maybe you can try again," she says with a little cough.

I cover a smile with my hand, and Mrs. Goldstein catches my eye and winks. Naomi looks at us, wide-eyed, and starts to giggle, and then we all burst out laughing. Soon I'm doubled over, hugging myself and howling with laughter—over this, and all my other sad, failed attempts at record-breaking. But as we laugh and laugh, everything is instantly better.

CHAPTER 13

* * *

"So now what?" Naomi wipes her eyes, which are watering from laughing. Or crying. Or both.

"Maybe we should have some rugelach?" I suggest.

That sets us off on another giggling spree.

"We made a bunch of the regular-sized ones that I took to your house," Naomi says. She pulls the top off a container on the counter and hands it to me. "Try some."

I choose a crescent-shaped pastry with strawberry jam inside and take a bite. It's flaky, sweet, buttery, and delicious.

"Yum!" I say. "I would totally eat your almost-world-record-breaking cookie if it hadn't turned into a burnt pancake."

"Me too." Naomi takes a bite of a chocolate-filled cookie. "In my old neighborhood there was a Jewish bakery that had even better rugelach than these. We rode bikes there, and the owner gave us free samples all the time."

"You could bike to stores?" In our neighborhood we can get to a couple of parks by bike, but the closest store requires crossing a highway ramp, so I'm not allowed.

"Yeah. My friends and I used to bike all over town . . . and play together every day." Naomi looks down and picks at the rest of the cookie lying on her napkin.

"Why'd you move?"

"My grandma lives alone over in Leisure World, and we wanted to be closer to her."

"Oh," I say, thinking of how much Naano hates to be at home by herself for longer than a few hours. "So that's good, right?"

"It's nice to see her more. And everyone says I'll get

used to living somewhere else . . . eventually." As her lip trembles, it's obvious that Naomi misses her friends, and her old home, a whole lot. And it hits me that I might have brought over cookies to welcome her family on the day they moved in, but I haven't been very welcoming ever since.

I take a deep breath and swallow the rest of my cookie, along with my big plans.

"Do you want to break a world record together?" I offer.

"Like what?" Naomi brightens a bit. "Should we bake a giant challah?"

"Um, maybe we should try something besides baking. What else are you good at?"

Naomi ponders the question. "I play the piano a little. I can do a headstand. And I'm practicing a bunch of magic tricks."

I want to see her magic tricks but don't know how they would work for breaking a record. Unless Naomi is pulling the largest number of bunnies out of a hat or sawing the biggest number of people in half. And if she's got a saw in her hand, I want nothing to do with breaking that record.

"How long can you do a headstand for?" I ask.

"Maybe a minute."

"Could you do it for a few hours?"

"I don't think so. All my blood rushes to my head. And I thought you said you wanted to do something together?"

"True."

"How about playing the longest game of freeze tag? Or roller Frisbee? Or doing a crab walk for a mile? Or fitting the most people into the cool tub?" Naomi's ideas flow out of her like she doesn't have to try to think of them. I've never heard of roller Frisbee and imagine all sorts of collisions and skinned knees. But I don't share that.

"Let's go outside and decide," I say.

"Should we ask everyone else to help us?" Naomi says.

"We can, if you want," I say. Although, the truth is, I'm still not sure how to feel about Gloria and Jade. Or about how they were so quick to ditch me and pick Naomi.

But as soon as we open the door, the two of them are already standing there about to ring the doorbell.

CHAPTER 14

* * *

"What are you doing?" Gloria asks. She seems startled to see me coming out of Naomi's house. "Want to play?"

"We're breaking a world record," Naomi shares.

"The same one as before?" Jade picks up the Hula-Hoop I left outside the front door, and inspects the dent.

"No." I reach for the hoop. "A different one."

"I can't believe Zayd ran right into you." Gloria sighs. "He needs to put those training wheels back on."

"I know," I agree. "I'm still mad at him."

"So, what record are you going to break, then?" Jade asks.

"We're still deciding," Naomi says. "What do you think we should do?"

"I don't know. Want to go to the clubhouse?" Jade suggests. "And make a list on the whiteboard? We can decide what everyone is doing. And design matching T-shirts—"

"How about we just get started?" I interrupt. "We don't need to do all that."

Jade's eyes narrow. "I thought you like to make rules," she says, and scowls.

"I do," I say, before adding: "Wait. What?"

"You always have a million rules for every game we play, Zara." Jade crosses her arms.

"Not a million," I protest. My voice is tiny, though, like it doesn't believe my words. I remind myself that Mr. Chapman said I ruled with fairness and grace. But as Jade glowers at me, I can't help but wonder, was he wrong?

"I make rules so we don't fight. And I thought you two liked my ideas," I protest weakly. "At least you *used* to. Before."

"What's that supposed to mean?" Jade scoffs.

"Yeah, before what?" Gloria looks puzzled.

"I mean, it just seems like neither of you wants to do anything I pick lately," I mutter.

"Well, sometimes other people have good ideas too," Jade insists.

I gulp and study my shoe, not sure how to respond. My throat starts to tighten, and my face grows warm. Maybe I got this all wrong, and *I'm* the reason why my friends rushed to play with Naomi. Do they think I'm too bossy? Do they view me as some kind of *evil* Queen of the Neighborhood?

"Zara was just helping me come up with good ideas before we came outside," Naomi says, jumping in. She comes closer to me and gives me a little nudge with her elbow. "Right, Zara?"

"I guess," I mumble. I want to believe her, but now I can't remember. *Was* I?

"Like what?" Jade asks.

"Like trying to break a record of something that I'm good at," Naomi says. "Or something that we can do together. All of us. Like setting the world record for the longest game of freeze tag ever."

"Really?" Jade asks.

"Yeah," Naomi says. "Zara just wants everyone to have fun. Right?"

"Right," I quickly add. "I mean, that's totally why I make rules and stuff."

We all turn to face Jade. She waves her hand around, like she's pushing away the bad feelings hanging in the air.

"It's all good," she says. "You're fine, Zara."

"Okay, then. Can we *please* do something now? I'm bored," Gloria continues. "Just pick something already."

"Do you want to all try to break that freeze tag record first?" Naomi suggests. She looks back and forth between all of us, like she isn't sure who to ask.

"Sure," Gloria replies first.

"Fine with me," I add.

"Okay," Jade agrees.

"We need to time ourselves, and make the teams fair," I start to say, and then pause. "I mean, if you're all okay with that. . . ."

"Sounds good," Naomi says.

"I think maybe we should video record our game too," Jade adds.

"Good idea," I say. And I mean it. It really is a smart idea.

"I'll go get my dad's iPad," Jade says. "And his tripod."

"All right, then. Let's get everyone else too, and go break this record," Naomi says. "And we are going to break it this time for sure, right, team?"

"Right!" Gloria cheers.

Jade pumps her fist with determination and smiles at me.

And just like that, I realize I'm sharing the crown. But, surprisingly, it makes me feel a lot lighter than I expected.

CHAPTER 15

* * *

Jade is frozen by the crab apple tree. Melvin is a statue by the sewer cover. And Naomi is lying like a dead body in the grass, where she fell and got tagged by Alan. Gloria is hovering dangerously close to Mr. Chapman's favorite bed of gigantic roses.

WHACK! Alan dives and tags Gloria on the foot, and she howls as she grabs a bush and touches a thorn.

"Ow! Okay, you got me!"

Alan is really good at being "it." And now he has tagged everyone except for me. I'm hanging out by the fence, while Alan catches his breath.

"Unfreeze me," Jade yells to me. "Quick!"

Alan is way too close to her, and I won't be able to get to Jade without being tagged. My best bet is to try to reach Melvin. Luckily, we decided the rule would be unfreezing by double high-fiving. Some people play that you have to crawl through the frozen person's legs to unfreeze them. But Melvin is so tiny, there's no way I would fit.

I make my move and start to run toward Jade. Then I suddenly turn around and dash in the other direction. Melvin's eyes grow rounder as I approach him. He stretches his hand toward me.

WHACK!

I feel a slap on my back. It's Alan. And now I'm frozen.

"I win!" Alan whoops and then does a victory dance.

"Not really, Alan," I grumble. "The goal wasn't to win. We were trying to have the *longest* game of freeze tag in history, remember? And that only lasted eighteen minutes."

"I can't help it if I'm too good," Alan says as he smirks, still dancing.

"I think we need more players," Naomi suggests. "To

make the game longer. We should get Michael and Zayd."

I bristle at the mention of Zayd. I'm still angry at him.

"Gloria! Jade!" Mrs. Thomas calls from their window. "Dinner!"

"We have to go," Gloria says.

"What about the record?" I ask.

"Maybe we can try tomorrow," Jade suggests as she runs home.

"I'm going in too." Alan walks away. "I'm hungry, and it's burger night."

"Can I move now?" Melvin asks. He's still frozen. I don't think he understands how this game works.

"Go home, Melvin," I say. "The game's over."

"Did we make the record?" he asks eagerly.

"Not yet. But we will." I look over at Naomi and give her a weak smile that shows how unsure about that I am.

"We will," she promises. "See you later."

I trudge back home and am greeted by a pungent odor and a big commotion in the kitchen.

"I don't know how I did that. I never forget!" Naano is wringing her hands and frowning.

"It's okay, Ami," Mom soothes. "It happens."

"What happened?" I ask.

"Naano forgot to turn off a pot on the stove, and the food burned," Zayd says. He looks at me nervously, but I pretend not to see or hear him. He's not getting off my enemy list without a serious apology.

"Maybe I can still save it," Mama says. She dumps the contents of the pot into a bowl as Naano shakes her head.

"No, no, no, it's ruined," Naano moans.

Nana Abu shuffles into the kitchen and sniffs the bowl. "She's right. It's no good," he says.

"I can go out and pick something up," Jamal Mamoo offers.

"Pizza?" Zayd asks.

"No, no, I'm sure we have something in the freezer," Mama says. "Zara, can you please go wash up?" She gives me her *You've been outside and have that summer stench* look.

I'm happy to leave, because the kitchen smells way worse

than I do. Zayd starts to follow me, but I ignore him, close the bathroom door, and take a long time scrubbing my hands and face with lots of foamy soap. When I finally come out and go to my room, I notice right away that it's different.

Did someone *clean* it for me while I was outside?

All my pillows and stuffed animals are neatly arranged on my bed. The worn pajamas and laundry I left on the floor are put away. My books are in a tidy stack. And even my slippers are lined up together by my closet.

The postcard from Mr. Chapman is lying on top of my bed. It says GREETINGS FROM JACKSONVILLE, FLORIDA with a photo of palm trees and a nice beach. On the other side, Mr. Chapman wrote in neat print:

Dear Zara and Zayd,

Thinking of you in Florida. I hope the new

neighbors are settling in and that you are

making friends. It's peaceful here, but I miss our

neighborhood and you, my young friends, most of

all. It will take time to adjust to life here. Come

visit soon and go fishing with me. Stay well and be happy. Give my best to your grandparents.

Yours,

Mr. Chapman

As I read it, I can't help but wonder if Mr. Chapman thinks of us the way Naomi thinks of her old friends. And I hope that someone is making him feel welcome in his new home. I decide I'm going to send him a letter and tell him about our plans, and ask Jade to help me make a nice card for everyone to sign for him.

There's another paper underneath the postcard, folded in half. I open it up and find a colorful drawing in marker. Four stick figures are standing in a line: Baba, Mama, me, and Zayd. I only know who's who because each of us is labeled. We are all holding hands, and there's grass under our feet and a big sun in the corner, with rays that almost reach our heads. I have a gigantic Hula-Hoop around my waist. And a splash of uneven letters in seven-year-old handwriting across the top reads:

Sorry, Zara. I Love You. —*Zayd*

I stare at his words, and at how gigantic my head is in the drawing. Slowly the bits of anger that were still floating around inside me fizzle out like flat soda. And then there's a tap on my door. It's Naano, watching me with a sly smile.

CHAPTER 16

* * *

"Hi, Naano," I say as I fold the drawing shut.

"Do you like the picture?" Naano comes in and slowly lowers herself onto the bed next to me.

"It's cute." I pause. "Wait. Did *you* tell him to do this?"

"Maybe."

"And to clean my room?"

"You think he cleans without someone telling him?" Naano snorts.

I can't imagine that at all.

"Thanks," I say, surprised.

"Zayd is a good boy, but sometimes he is a budhoo," Naano continues. "He's going to be eight soon and he still can't ride a bicycle?"

"I didn't learn until I was around his age," I say, remembering.

"You? I don't think so." Naano shakes her head.

"I'm pretty sure," I say. "Alan and I were learning at the same time, even though he's younger, and he learned first."

"I Iшшmph."

We sit in silence for a minute, and I start to feel warm as Naano studies my face and adjusts the thin scarf that covers her hair. Am I supposed to do something else? Does she expect me to say sorry too, for getting upset earlier? Because I still believe what I said: Naano does take Zayd's side all the time.

"You know, Zara, you are my big girl," Naano finally says, like she's reading my mind. "Zayd is the baby, and he is still learning. The way he doesn't eat anything with any taste and makes such a fuss. I love my skinny mouse, but he can be . . . kya kehte hein . . . a pain in the neck."

I giggle at Naano uttering those unexpected last words, which sound extra funny in her accent, even if they are true. Naano chuckles too.

"When he sits with his white rice and his white pasta, taking all day to eat, I want to yell at him sometimes. But he is little."

"I know, Naano."

"And I see how he bothers you. But he wants to be just like you. You are his hero."

"I guess." I mean, I can see that.

"You know, you remind me of me, when I was a girl like you," Naano continues.

"I do?"

Naano reaches out and gently touches the crown charm hanging around my neck, the one Mr. Chapman gave me. "When I was growing up in Lahore, I was the leader of all my cousins and played outside all day too."

"You did?"

"Yes, I was a Girl Guide," Naano says proudly. "And captain of my netball team. And I could arm wrestle kids older than me and beat them."

I try to imagine a girl version of my grandmother. But just like with the Hula-Hoop, it's hard to picture. Especially the arm wrestling.

"And like you, I always wanted to win. After I came to America too. Do you know I won a contest for making the best biryani on Pakistan Day?" Naano continues.

"You did?" I haven't heard this story before.

"Yes. There were six different people in the contest who cooked their very best biryani. And judges who picked the winner. I was worried because I thought I'd added too much water and that my rice would be mushy. But it was perfect, and everyone was amazed by the good taste. The best part was, I beat that Shagufta Chaudhry, who everyone always said was such a good cook." Naano gushes as she reminisces about this most wonderful day.

"What's Pakistan Day?" I ask.

"You don't remember a few years ago when we went to the fairgrounds, where there was a music performance of tabla and sitar, and all those food stalls, and you got those tiny Pakistani flags?"

"I remember it a little. We still have the flags in the toy box downstairs. But I didn't know you won anything."

"Not just *anything*. The blue ribbon, for beating that Shagufta Chaudhry," Naano repeats, and I decide that Shagufta Chaudhry must be her sworn enemy. "And maybe

I should be in your big book too, for making the best biryani in the world."

"Hold on. You want to be in the Guinness World Records?"

"Why not?" Naano says. "If you help me, I can do it. Even though I burned the food today like a silly old fool."

"I don't know, Naano. I haven't had good luck breaking any records. And I'm not sure that having the best-tasting biryani can be a record."

"You will find a way," Naano says. She puts her arm around me and gives me a squeeze. "You are my smart girl."

I look at Naano, unsure if she's serious or teasing. But either way, the apology I was holding back flows out.

"Sorry for saying that stuff before, Naano."

"It's okay. Sometimes smart girls act butthameez."

I giggle again, this time because she said Zayd's and my favorite Urdu word. I mean, it has the word "butt" in it, after all, which gets him into hysterics every time. And then Naano shakes her head, takes my hand, and commands, "Help me get up. It's time to eat."

CHAPTER 17

✳ ✳ ✳

"What is this?" I use a piece of naan to poke at the meat covered in gravy on my plate.

"It's a korma, left over from Eid. From the freezer, Zara. Eat it," Mama orders, and I can tell that between Zayd's crying and the burnt food, she is not in the mood for whining.

There's some fat stuck to the chunk of meat, and I try to pull it off. It makes me gag.

"Stop picking, Zara, and eat your food properly," Baba says.

"What about him?" I point to Zayd, who is sitting in front of a plate of plain rice with some naan on the side. "He's not eating it."

"I give up." Mama sighs. "Some battles aren't worth fighting. He'll eat when he eats."

Naano isn't ready to surrender, though. She cuts up some meat into tiny pieces and slips them onto Zayd's plate.

Jamal Mamoo chuckles. "She used to do that with me when I was little," he says. "I sat for hours with my food. Everyone said I was going to win the Guinness World Record for sitting at the table with my dinner the longest."

"You can break a record for doing that?" Zayd's eyes grow bigger. "I'm so going to win!"

"Look what you started," Mama scolds. "As if he wasn't slow enough already without you encouraging him."

Zayd gets up, runs to get Jamal Mamoo's old book from the family room, and lugs it to the table. Then he grins at me. I told him I liked his drawing before we sat down to eat, and he gave me a half hug, so we're good again.

"Zayd, what are you doing?" Baba complains. "Sit down and eat your dinner, please."

"Why don't you let the boy read if he wants?" Nana Abu interrupts, his voice gentle. "He can nourish his mind and body at the same time. I used to read with my meals when I was a student."

Zayd takes a minuscule bite of rice and chews as he flips through the pages of the book that's resting on his lap. I find a piece of meat without any fat and nibble on it.

"Hey, Zara. Did you know that you need to get permission to break a record?" Zayd asks after a few minutes of quiet eating.

"What?" I flip my head around to look at Jamal Mamoo, who drops his fork.

"And you need to fill out a form if you want your record to count," Zayd continues, pointing to the page.

"Are you serious?" I get up, stand behind Zayd, and look over his shoulder to read a section all the way in the back of the book entitled "How to Break a Guinness World Record."

"OH MY GOSH! It's true, Mamoo! There's a whole

application . . . and you have to be approved before you can break a record. And then there have to be . . . official witnesses, too? Why didn't you tell us?"

"I guess I never read to the end of the book." Jamal Mamoo smiles sheepishly. "But now that I think of it, that totally makes sense."

"Why?" I demand.

Jamal Mamoo clears his throat. "Well, first of all, let's agree that it's not really my fault. If it was so easy to break a record, it wouldn't be a big deal. And second of all, I thought you'd have fun with this thing, not turn it into a major high-stakes drama."

"It's not just me! Everyone wants to break a record now," I explain, clutching his arm. "All the kids in the neighborhood, and even *Naano*."

"Naano? Really?" Jamal Mamoo laughs. "For what?"

"Don't you laugh, butthameez. I have a blue ribbon!" Naano pipes up from across the table.

"For your biryani? That was a great day. You showed that Shagufta Chaudhry," Nana Abu adds. He beams at Naano, who glows from the praise of ruthlessly crushing

her competition. For a second I wonder what happened to this Shagufta Auntie after she lost the ribbon, and whether or not she and Naano could have ever been friends if they hadn't been trying to outdo each other. But then I turn back to the current situation.

"So, what are we supposed to do now?" I press my uncle.

"I don't know," Jamal Mamoo admits.

I glare at him. This is not helping one bit.

"I'm sure you will figure it out," Nana Abu says, and smiles at me from across the table.

"We can help you, Zara," Zayd volunteers.

"And remember, no matter what you do, you'll always hold the record in our hearts," Baba adds.

Everyone groans when he says that, and Baba puts up both his hands. "What?"

"That's super corny, man." Jamal Mamoo shakes his head.

Baba grins. "It's true."

As I look around at my family, I realize that Baba is onto something. And a new idea pops into my head.

CHAPTER 18

* ❋ *

The next day I find an old composition book on my bookshelf and rip out the used pages in the front. I don't need sloppy journal entries from when I was in second grade. There! It's as good as new. Then I take a marker and print a few words across the cover in my neatest handwriting.

It's a sunny and humid morning as I head across the street and knock on the Goldsteins' front door. Michael opens it up.

"Hey." He nods when he sees me. "Naomi's eating

breakfast. I already told her I'm not playing in any marathon freeze tag game or timing how long I can run backward. But if you want to play regular football or soccer, I'm in."

"Got it." I smile.

Naomi comes to the door, holding a half-eaten bagel with cream cheese on it. "Hi."

"Hi. Can you come out?"

"Sure." Naomi slips on some sandals that are lying by the door and comes out, still holding the bagel. "I have a bunch of new ideas for records we can try," she says. "Like sewing the longest friendship bracelets or walking the most dogs at once. I was practicing juggling beanbags for, like, two hours in my room last night."

"That's great." I detect a tiny cream cheese mustache on Naomi's upper lip. "But I have some bad news."

"What?"

"You have to fill out a bunch of forms and get your idea approved to break a Guinness World Record and get official permission."

"Oh." Naomi's mustache turns upside down.

"Plus, there are all these special rules to follow and you have to get witnesses."

Naomi flops down onto her front step and chews her bagel as she listens to the rest of the news.

"And it can take a really long time, like twelve weeks, to hear back," I say.

Naomi shoves the rest of the bagel into her mouth and wipes her mouth with the back of her hand. "So now what? Are we going to quit? After all that?" she asks, her face drooping.

"No." I hold up my notebook. "We can do something better. We can make our own neighborhood records!"

"Like what?"

"Like all the ones you just said, and any others. We can keep track of them here, in this notebook. And make awards or give out trophies too, if we want."

Naomi looks at the writing on my notebook, and I can see her mind working as she reads *"Brisk River Book of Neighborhood Records."*

"And the clubhouse?" she asks.

"It'll be our headquarters, and our Hall of Fame!"

Naomi jumps up. "That's so much better!" she cheers. "We don't have to follow rules, and this way everyone can win at something."

I bite my lip as she says the last part, because I honestly never thought about everyone else when I was busy trying to break a record. I was doing it alone, to be the best and get everyone to respect me as the Queen. But Naomi has always wanted to include everyone and have fun together.

"Let's get all the kids!" Naomi says. "You get Gloria and Jade, and I'll get Melvin and Alan."

"Don't forget Michael and Zayd," I add.

"I'm right here," a voice says. I look up, and it's Michael.

"I already told you I'm not doing that stuff," he says, looking bored in that way thirteen-year-olds do sometimes.

"But you can do whatever you want to get into our Hall of Fame," I explain.

"Hall of Fame? Like football?" Michael asks.

"Yup. But ours includes all of us, and any kinds of records we want to break."

"And cookies," Naomi adds.

"I'll think about it," Michael says, as if he seriously needs time to decide. But I can already tell, he's going to be with us.

CHAPTER 19

✳ ✳ ✳

Zayd runs out of our house, and I'm glad to see that this time he remembers to stop to look both ways before crossing the street. Then he makes a beeline to us, breathless, as the gang gathers on Naomi's lawn. Jade lugs over her whiteboard and a bunch of dry-erase markers. We huddle around the board while Gloria kneels on the grass and scribbles down all the things everyone yells out.

"I'm going to juggle a soccer ball at least fifty times," Alan says. "And after that I'll break my own record and get to a hundred."

"One record at a time, please," Gloria says. She makes columns for DATE, NAME, CATEGORY, RECORD and fills in the details. "Juggle fifty times" goes next to Alan's name in red marker.

"I'm going to climb that tree all the way to the top branches," Melvin says, pointing to the crab apple tree. "But someone has to give me a boost."

"You can't do anything dangerous, Melvin," I warn. "And you have to ask your mom." I glance at Jade because I just made another rule. But it is an old habit, and in this case I figure it's about safety first. She nods in agreement.

"I'm breaking the record for riding my bike with no hands!" Zayd declares next.

"Whoa, Zayd. Did you hear what your sister literally just said?" Jade warns. "How about you learn to ride your bike *with* your hands first?" We all laugh, including Zayd.

"Oh yeah! I need to do that," he jokes, before dramatically slapping himself on the head and falling onto the grass.

"I can't decide between juggling or the crab walk first," Naomi says to me.

"You've been working on the juggling, right? So that could be a good one to start with. Or maybe you could do one of your magic tricks."

"Right! My magic tricks." Naomi clasps her hands together. "I totally forgot I have a new one I want to show you all!"

"What are you going to do, Zara?" Zayd asks me.

"I'm going to try Hula-Hooping again. I was so close to reaching an hour before," I say. "But only if someone has a Hula-Hoop I can borrow, and you promise not to bump into me again."

"I think I have one," Alan says, and then he runs home to get it while Zayd promises to stay far away from me.

"I read that some people climb stairs while Hula-Hooping," Naomi mentions. "You could do that next."

"One at a time!" Gloria repeats as she writes down my goal.

"Wait. What are you and Jade doing?" I ask. "You didn't write down anything for yourself."

"I'm going to eat the most cookies in an hour," Gloria says, and grins.

"No fair, I was going to do that!" Jade protests.

"How about you do it together, and set the record for the most cookies eaten by sisters?" I suggest.

"That works," Jade says. And I know for sure that this time she doesn't mind that it's my idea at all.

Michael volunteers to film and time us, but I think he wants to watch and pretend he's not still thinking of a record of his own to break. He hasn't gone inside one time since we started all this, and I can tell he's having fun.

I offer to write all the official winners in my notebook and make us all certificates. They'll hang on the walls of the clubhouse. It doesn't have red carpets and chandeliers, but Jade managed to put up the string lights and some homemade curtains, and it's looking pretty fancy.

We spend the rest of the day working on each of our records, helping each other out, and cooling down with freeze pops during breaks. Naomi looks over at me and we exchange smiles when Michael sets an accidental record for getting a football stuck in the crab apple tree three times in a row. The third time, he and Alan kick his soccer ball at it to try to get the football out.

"Stop it! You're going to hit me!" a squeaky voice yelps.

It's Melvin, hidden behind the leaves.

"It sounds like the tree is talking to us." Naomi giggles and points.

As I laugh with my new friend, I feel a comforting squeeze in my heart, and it occurs to me that I had nothing to worry about. The New People turned out to be exactly the type of neighbors that all of us, including me, needed. And now I'm convinced that it's even better to be a member of an awesome gang of friends and a team of record breakers than it is to be the Queen. I'm pretty sure Mr. Chapman would agree.

Brisk River Book of Neighborhood Records

Date	Name	Category	Record
August 5	Alan	Most red freeze pops eaten in 24 hours	7 pops
August 5	Naomi	Most times not guessing the right card in magic trick	17 times
August 7	Michael	Longest time reciting Hebrew for bar mitzvah practice	2 hours
August 8	Zara	Longest time Hula-Hooping while juggling and chewing gum	13 seconds
August ~~8, 10,~~ 14	Alan	Number of times juggling soccer ball without dropping it	~~27 times~~ ~~36 times~~ 48 times
August 14	Jade	Fastest time making certificates with glitter writing for all the people breaking records so far	2 hours
August 17	Gloria	Longest time laughing while drinking water without spitting	8 seconds
August 17	Melvin	Highest jump to high-five Michael	8 inches
August 19	Zayd	Longest time to eat a grilled cheese sandwich	94 minutes
August 19	Naomi	Most times trying to break world record involving rugelach	3 times
August 19	Jade	Fastest time singing the alphabet backward	52 seconds

Acknowledgments

When I was a kid, my #1 rule for visiting the library was leaving with a book I knew I liked, along with new ones. I adored stories of family and friendship, set in homes and neighborhoods. And no one mastered those better than my favorite author, Beverly Cleary.

I wanted to be like Ramona Quimby, with her big heart, her silly antics, and even her grumpiness. She wasn't a perfect kid, but that made her relatable and hilarious. And I checked out her books, over and over.

My dream is to write a collection of books that kids can connect with in that same way. And I'm grateful that my editor, Kendra Levin, shares my vision for Zara's Rules. Zara's a girl with passion and plenty of interests who's trying to figure herself out, often through ridiculous plans. Thank you, Kendra, for embracing Zara and her family, and for all your help in bringing these stories to life.

An important rule in the book-making world is to make sure you have a great team. I've been fortunate to have a smart and supportive agent in Matthew Elblonk. My writing group, Joan Waites, Ann McCallum, and Laura Gehl, is always ready to drop everything to read my work and give me feedback. My friend Afgen Sheikh is a trusted sounding board. My brother Omar Khan is an incredibly careful reader. And of course, I'm indebted to Wastana Haikal for the super fun and lively art in these books, and to the dedicated crew at Simon & Schuster for all that they do to produce and promote them.

Another good rule when writing for children is to surround yourself with them. Big thanks to the many kids who share their thoughts and ideas, who write letters and encourage me. You are all champions, including my buddies Zara; Isa and Mikail Mirza; and Zayd Salahuddin. I'm also forever grateful to educators, parents, booksellers, and everyone else who shares my books with readers.

This series draws from my experiences with the best neighbors in the world. When the Pitch family moved in across the street, I didn't know that they would become lifelong friends and some of the most important people in my life. Thank you, Nomi, Michael, Marion, and Tony for being such a central and unforgettable part of my child-hood. Tony, you are missed.

My family rules my heart and is a big part of this series. My brave and brilliant parents inspired Naano and Nana Abu, my tall and goofy brothers remind me of Jamal Mamoo, and my creative and crafty sister is basically Gloria and Jade in one person. Finally, my loving husband and two incredible sons keep breaking their own records: just when I think I can't possibly love you more or be prouder, you prove me wrong.

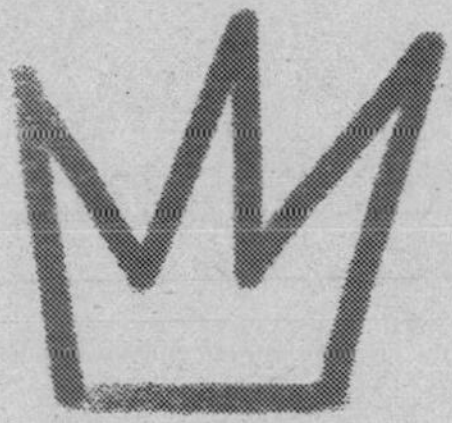